KATHLEEN AND THE COMMUNION COPTER

By

Avril O'Reilly

PUBLISHED BY:

Avril O'Reilly on Lulu

*****

Many thanks to Connie Keefe.

She always liked my writing.

*****

ISBN 978-1-291-51674-6

Contents

Chapter 1

Patrick's Street

Kathleen and Nan Knowles were standing on Patrick's Street watching a man doing a huge drawing on the pavement. "Oh, Kathleen" said Nan "If I had a wall big enough I'd take that home. That's pure art." It was a drawing of angels in Communion dresses flying over Cork city.

Nan and Kathleen were in town to see what they could find for Kathleen to wear for her First Holy Communion. It was not until May but the school had already started doing special classes and masses. Nan had decided that the ladies of the family should put some thought and attention into the clothing for the day. Kathleen had stayed in Nan and Granddad Knowles' house the night before and now they were waiting for mum to join them.

"Time's moving on." said Nan scrolling through numbers on her phone. "I wonder where your mum is. It's not like her to be late for a shopping trip. "

Kathleen could tell from Nan's voice that she was leaving a message. "We're outside Cashes just across from Cudmores" she was saying. She always called shops by their old names. Cashes was now called BT's and Cudmores was Cael's Nails. "What's Cudmores?" Kathleen asked. "The loveliest grocers in Cork. I wish I could show you the beautiful displays of fruits and sweets they used to do. This time of year they would have Christmas cakes and...oh it's your mum." She sounded delighted but her expression changed quickly. "There's a problem with your brothers." she whispered while mum's voice squeaked through the phone. Tommy and Teddy were six and three and a bit. They were troublesome, even when they weren't trying to be. "Teddy is where?" Nan was saying "A gymkhana? In Belgooly? Chasing a horsebox? Why?"

"Oh, dear." said Nan "We have a problem. Your dad went to the garage for milk with Teddy. There were horseboxes parked at the garage and Teddy is after climbing into one. The horsebox drove off and now your dad is chasing it in his car. Your mum thinks they're going to a gymkhana in Belgooly and now she has to mind Tommy."

"That poor horse." said Kathleen "I bet he had his vuvuzela with him." "Do you mean that noisy horn thing he's always blowing into?" asked Nan. "I hope the horse stands on it." "But what about our shopping trip?" asked Kathleen in a worried voice " Mum is the shopping expert." "We'll just do it ourselves" said Nan firmly.

"We'll be fine. Let's go to the Kylemore first for a cake and we'll make our plan." Nan was great at making nice things happen.

They got a good table in the Café Kylemore, looking over Patrick's Street, and sat down with a chocolate eclair for Kathleen and a low fat blueberry muffin for Nan. Nan Knowles took out her special notebook. Her notebook was full of things to do; all crossed out when she had done them. Kathleen thought it was like a magic book. Whatever got written down always got crossed out. If Nan wrote "Must fly to the moon on an elephant" Kathleen was sure that it was only a matter of time before the words were crossed out and Nan and her elephant were on the front of the Irish Examiner as the first pair from Cork to make a moon landing.

"Alright." said Nan taking out her pen "Find Kathleen a dress she loves" she said aloud while writing in her book. "We'll make appointments on Shandon Street, appointments on Castle Street and in the Moderne." "What are appointments?" Kathleen asked. "Well, when the dresses and veils and tiaras come in we tell the shops what day and time we want to come in to see what they have. Then we go in and you'll try on the whole rig out. It takes quite a while and you'll be the centre of attention."

"So am I not fitting on any dresses today?" asked Kathleen disappointed. "Well, the dresses won't really be in the shops til after Christmas," Nan explained. Kathleen couldn't stop her face from looking sad. "But I have an idea." said Nan. We can see if there are any flower girl dresses in Roches." It was called Debenhams now but Nan had been very fond of Roches and she hadn't ever warmed to the new name.

"Nan, doesn't mum like Communion dresses?" asked Kathleen thoughtfully. "Of course she does, why do you say that?" asked Nan. "Well, when Tommy was in the Christmas nativity play being a shepherd mum made him a Pinterest board of shepherd costumes. But she never made me a Communion one" "Is that like a pin-cushion?" asked Nan looking puzzled. "No, Nan!" Kathleen giggled. "It's on the computer. You get lots of pictures from the internet and you put them all together on a board on a special website." "Isn't that great?" said Nan, impressed, "I suppose it's like a scrapbook. I used to do a scrapbook of pretty dresses when I was your age. I used to cut them out of magazines." She picked up her special notebook. "Learn to work Pinterest" she said while writing firmly.

They came down the escalators. They had a quick look into Dunnes but it was all Christmas party dresses. Debenhams didn't have any dresses either. Nan bought some bubble baths to keep everyone's spirits up. She bought lavender for herself and a My Little Kitten Karate Princess Banan-o-Mango one for Kathleen. "Isn't it dotie?" said Nan "The bottle is shaped like a kitten in pyjamas. Marvellous." "Nan, not pyjamas! It's a karategi" said Kathleen.

Nan looked at her watch. "Come on love, grab onto your kitten. Let's go to work."

Chapter 2

Fitting On

As they marched along Patrick's Street, on their way to make appointments, Kathleen spotted something. "What about that dress?" she said pointing at a sparkly pretty dress with white embroidered swirls. "Is a Monsoon dress holy enough?" "It certainly is." said Nan "And we can always get Father Hearty to bless it for you. Would you like to fit it on?" In they went, smiling with excitement.

While Kathleen went into the changing rooms Nan chatted to the shop assistant. The girl had long curly red hair and very long orange fingernails. When Kathleen came out Nan and the girl gave her a round of applause. "You look beautiful" said Nan. "And very holy." added the girl, whose name badge said Karen. Kathleen smiled happily. "What about a tiara?" asked Karen. "Would you like to try sparkly or flowery?" "Flowery, please." said Kathleen "Do you have any with roses on them?" The girl flicked through the rail of tiaras with her long orange nails and found a delicate pretty band. She put it carefully on Kathleen's head. Tiny gems at the centre of each rose twinkled under the shop lights. "Wow!" said Kathleen with a huge smile "I'm holy and sparkly."

As they headed out of the shop Nan caught the shop girl's eye. They gave each other a nod and a wink.

"That's a good start." said Nan. Next month town will be full of dresses, gloves, umbrellas and all sorts of things. You'll be spoiled for choice. We'll head for North Main Street now."

After making their appointments they did a quick dash into the charity shops because Nan was addicted to them. They came out with two romances, a Barbie for Kathleen and trucks for Tommy and Teddy. "Five euro!" said Nan who loved getting a bargain. "We forgot Dad." said Kathleen. "I never know what your father likes" was the reply. "Dad likes boring things". said Kathleen. "See that book about engines there for 50 cents? He'd like that".

Back in they went for the boring present and came back out with the book, a wedding dress for Barbie, an ornamental bird for Granddad and two more romances. "I think we're done now." said Nan. "The car is nearby so we might as well head home.

When they got home Dad was in the drive vacuuming straw out of his car. It smelt like a stable. "I'll kill Teddy." said Dad. "Please do." said Kathleen "He's a pest."

Mum answered the door. "Did ye have a good day?" she asked while everyone hugged hello. Teddy was hopping up and down shouting "Nagazine! Nagazine!" Tommy was staring hopefully at Nan's bag. Nan handed out her charity shop presents while mum urged everyone to move into the living room.

"Come on" said Mum "What are we all doing out here in the hall? Tommy, stop doing that with the truck and tell your dad to come in for a cup of tea. Sit down everyone. I'll bring in biscuits." Everyone moved towards the living room. "Thanks for the books." said mum. "Kathleen, that's a sweet kitten. What lovely pyjamas." "Tut tut " said Nan "Not pyjamas. A karategi!".

There was a surprise. "Teddy has a present for you, Kathleen" said mum. We stopped in a garage to clean him up and he got you a magazine of Communion dresses. "Nagazine" he said proudly handing Kathleen a battered magazine. He had dropped it a few times and spilt Ribena on it but it was glossy and shiny and full of photos. "Wow, Teddy, thanks" Kathleen said "You can have some of my Banan-o-Mango bubble bath. It'll stop you smelling like a horse."

Chapter 3

The Communion Copter

All of the children were working hard on their preparations. On top of all the prayers and hymns they had to learn everyone had their own individual concerns.

Ellie was worried about her sins. All of the children were learning about reconciliation which is about saying sorry properly. Father Hearty, the priest, was doing confessions. Ellie's problem was that she was a naturally nice girl. Also she had no baby brothers to bring out her dark side. The other children were sharing their sins with her.

Áine was worried that her little brother Olan would be unable to stop talking in the church. He was a gifted child so he had difficulty shutting up. Maria was trying to teach her big sisters to do movie star smiles. "I want my Communion photos to look nice but Dad says my sisters always look like they are chewing sour wasps in photos.

Jack and Luke, the identical twins, were trying to grow their hair long to create a special hairstyle. Maureen was trying to gain weight to fit into the dress her cousin was lending her. Damien wanted to draw a special picture for the church. His favourite thing to draw was the Baby Jesus but he was worried that that might be only for Christmas.

Samantha was very worried about clothes. "I have no dresses." she told Kathleen anxiously. "Can I borrow one from you, please? We're the same size." "There's no need to worry about that at all." said Kathleen. "This is what happens. Your mum and you go shopping and she picks you a nice one. You wear it in the church and keep it clean. You might need to wear it again to visit people. When you get home from the church you put on ordinary clothes for the bouncy castle".

Samantha looked even more worried now. "But where will I get a bouncy castle?" she asked looking even more stressed. "Um. They just come on the day." said Kathleen reassuringly. "A man brings one and puts it in your garden. It just comes."

Kathleen was excited about her dress. She was telling Maureen about the tasteful dress her mum had promised her. "What does tasteful mean, asked Maureen. You can't taste a dress, can you?" "I am not sure." said Kathleen. "I think tasteful means really beautiful and sparkling like an angel or a saint would have. Or maybe a princess."

Nessa wanted very much to show off. Nessa's dad was rich. He made special effects for singers who were appearing in the Eurovision Song Contest. Say if a singer wanted to appear to fly across the stage or if a pop group wanted to appear out of a basket of fire or a waterfall then Nessa's dad was the man for the job. He had loads of money and was always buying Nessa gifts. But no matter what he gave her she was never happy for long and usually had a sour puss on her half an hour after getting her latest present. Kathleen had never seen Nessa's dad smile.

Nessa was smiling today because her dad had promised her a Communion Copter to fly her to the church. He was going to get her a little white helicopter and have it painted in whatever style she wanted. "Yesterday I told him to paint me as a fairy on the sides but then I told him to paint over that and to paint me as a mermaid. But I think tonight I'll tell him to paint over that and have me sitting on a unicorn" she explained to anyone who would listen to her.

"Come on, children" said Miss Cronin the teacher "It's time for the practice mass."

The whole class and Miss Cronin were walking across to the schoolyard to meet their parents for the practice mass. "Why do we need practice masses?" Samantha asked Kathleen. "I think it's to teach the parents how to behave themselves in a church. " replied Kathleen "Like, say if your mum's phone rang and she went 'Hey, Girl' out loud. You'd be mortified. Or if your dad was trying to watch a football match on an iPhone and he shouted GOOOOAL. "

The children were filing in. Jack and Luke were singing. Jack did a cartwheel on the carpet. Nessa was showing off her new rosary beads. She was twirling them around and round. Maureen was eating an iced bun.

Father Hearty came out of the sacristy. He stood on the altar looking around. He seemed to be confused. He stared at the mob of children and parents in front of him "Can anyone help me?" he asked "Am I in my church at all?"

He looked around. "I seem to have wandered into a shopping centre. Just in case anyone isn't sure this is a Church! Don't mind looking for the soft play area or the café. In the House of God there's no free WiFi internet access so I'll ask ye all to please switch off any PadFones, iPads, Phablets and tablets. There were sounds of shuffling and clicking as everyone complied.

Father Hearty scanned the congregation. "Did I see two fellas cartwheeling in here?" Jack held up his hand and prodded Luke to do the same. "Is it Jedward I have here? Well, I'm sorry, Jedward, but this is a church not the stage of the Cork Opera House. Less of the gymnastics, please lads." He spotted Maureen. "Maureen, is that an iced bun you're eating?" Maureen's mum grabbed the bun and hid it in her bag.

"Here's Mr and Mrs Crowley. We had little Billy Crowley in for his First Holy Communion last year….maybe he'll drop in some day for his second Holy Communion. And Nessa…has anyone seen Nessa's horse? Horse anyone? She's waving her rosary beads like a lasso…must be hoping to rope a horse or a bullock?"

"Mrs Shea. Aren't you looking well? You're as lovely as you were on your wedding day when I last saw you. Oh, and there's Mr Shea. Isn't that great. I thought the pair of ye had emigrated."

"Now, a show of hands. How many of ye have been in a church before?" Just over half the hands went up. Parents were heard whispering "You were here for your Christening." and a few more hands shot into the air. Father Hearty nodded. "Is there anyone here knows how to bless themselves?" He surveyed the crowd. "Oh Sweet Divine Mother of God, we're back to basics with this shower. Alright, everyone copy me". He raised his hand to his forehead then paused. "I should say ye are all as welcome as the flowers in May. God loves a full house. Now copy me…In the Name of the Father…."

Chapter 4

The Trip to Bandon

Kathleen, her mum and Nan Knowles were on their way to Bandon in the car. Mum was driving. "I think we might find something tasteful for the Communion if we avoid the city centre." she said confidently.

They were not even sure if Bandon had dress shops but it was nice to go for a spin anyway. There were plenty of interesting looking shops on the main street.

They started in YoungWear. They looked at a rail full of dresses. "Nan," said Kathleen "Did you have a mini or a maxi for your Communion Day?" "A maxi" said Nan "but it turned into a mini. My dress was made of crochet and a thread came loose. When I walked up the aisle it unraveled itself. It started out at my ankles and ended up by my knees! Lucky that my teacher saw it or I would have been at the altar in my slip!" They all laughed at the thought of Nan receiving Communion in her undies.

In Kevin Bowen's clothes shop Nan got distracted by Cotton Rich Executive Socks for Granddad. Mum started to look a bit stressed. She always got stressed when Nan was shopping for bargains and cheap things made out of nylon. "I'll just pop across the road for a moment." she said and hurried off to look at shoes. Kathleen looked around Kevin Bowens. There were no dresses here at all. She found a shelf full of scented candles and started sniffing them. Nan got her a vanilla one.

They met up in Crowley Calnan clothes shop. Mum was holding a lace handkerchief. It was tiny and cost twenty euro. "Isn't that divine?"

she said happily. She was always happy around expensive things.

Kathleen had found a brochure full of pictures of girls in fancy clothes having picnics and smiling. "Can I have this, please?" she asked the shop assistant. "Of course you can, girl" was the reply. Nan pointed out that none of the dresses in the shop was white so they headed back out.

Mum looked thoughtful.."I wonder would we have been nearly better off in town." she said. "I'll ring Emer".   They drifted across the road and ended up in a shoe shop. Mum picked her mobile phone out of her bag "Emer" she said "Do you know if Noa Noa has communion dresses?" There was a pause and she shook her head. "Well, is there anything nice in BT's?" There was another pause. "Do you still have the address of that Swedish website that makes hats out of recycled paper?" She spotted what Kathleen and Nan were

looking at and looked shocked. "Kathleen, no!.
Not crocs for a Holy Communion! And Mam!
You can't buy MBTs. So unstylish. Oh, Emer,
are these two related to me at all?"

Nan's phone started to ring. Kathleen held
her umbrella and shopping bags while Nan rooted
in her handbag. Twenty rings later Nan answered.
"Teddy is where?!" she shrieked. She waved at
mum to hang up and thrust the phone at her.
"Teddy is stuck in the dishwasher!!" Mum
grabbed the phone and listened as Dad explained.

"What was he doing in the dishwasher?' said
Mum anxiously. She hung up and told Kathleen
and Nan what Dad had said. "Tommy told him
there was hidden treasure in the cutlery holder and
now his foot is stuck in the fork holder. The
firemen are on the way."

She clicked the phone shut. "We'd better go
home." she said sadly. Kathleen was not so sure.

"Mum," she said "I bet the kitchen floor is covered in dirty plates" Tommy would have taken them out to make room for Teddy." Mum pursed her lips. "We really should go back." she said again but this time she did not sound quite so firm.

Two hours later they headed for the car park. Nan had a par of comfortable but fashionable bronze sandals. Mum had red leather high heels and Kathleen had three lollipops. Mum had bought her one and then Nan had slipped her two more.

They settled into the car for the trip home. Kathleen was sucking a green lollipop, looking at her book of pictures and sniffing her candle. Nan was taking all the shoes out of the bag to twirl them around and admire them. Mum looked happy. Maybe tomorrow we'll try Clonakilty.' she said.

Chapter 5

Online Shopping

Nan Knowles was coming around to help with the Communion dress shopping. Kathleen was sitting in the living room with her coat on waiting to hear Nan's car. Eventually she heard the beep of the car's horn and she ran for the front door.

"Oh, no coats needed." said Mum. "We are shopping online today. I've been making Pinterest boards of dresses and beads. Everything we need is in the computer." A shopping trip without cake stops was not what Nan and Kathleen had expected but they were open to new ideas. Mum led the way to her computer desk in the living room

Everyone gathered around the computer to see the dresses on the screen. A grid of photos appeared. Mum had obviously been working hard. "Ah, lovely." said Nan " A good slip is a very important purchase." "They aren't slips, Mam." said Mum, looking a little bit offended, "They are tasteful cotton dresses." Teddy came to have a look. "That's what Granddad wore when he was in hospital for his Whopperation". Mum was getting a little bit cross now. "Boys, this is not suitable for you. Go and get the coffee jar for Nan, will you, please?"

"Bags me carry the jar." said Teddy running off. "But I'm making the coffee" said Tommy chasing after him. Dad had bought a new machine for making coffee. There was a big jar full of tiny little coloured capsules with different flavours of coffee. If you put a capsule in the machine and put a cup in the right place under the spout you would get a perfect cup of coffee. Kathleen and Tommy were allowed to make drinks for visitors but Teddy was not. He was small and clumsy and he might scald himself and waste the coffee.

Mum and Kathleen and Nan stared at the computer. Mum was pointing at each dress in turn, clicking on the pictures to make them bigger and describing the different ones. Even though they all looked exactly the same Mum had something to say about each one. "This one is organic cotton from France. This cloth is hand weaved by women in Pakistan. This one is made from cotton that is grown without any pesticides." "Pesticides." said Nan. thoughtfully. "Are you sure about this, love? I think nowadays girls like a little bit of 'bling'. Isn't that what they call it?" "Well, I think these dresses are very elegant and demure." Mum replied.

Teddy came back with the jar. Tommy cleared his throat loudly. "Take your pick, Nan." He said grandly "We have a wide range of colours and flavours to suit every taste". Kathleen wished the same were true of the dresses. A wider range would have been nice but Mum had worked hard and Kathleen did not want to hurt her feelings.

"Are we going into town to look at more dresses?" she asked. "There's no need." said Mum "You just need to pick your favourite and it will be delivered to the door." "Right, so." Said Kathleen and looked again at the tasteful dresses and tried to make a selection. It was not easy. There were no special sleeves or beads or embroidered patterns to make one different from the others. "I'd like the one with….em, the one with……". It was a struggle but she had a bright idea …"the one with the…no pesticides, please!" "Oh, I like that one too. Good choice!" said Mum while clicking buttons. She hit the Enter key and said "There! It's on the way". "Thanks Mum' said Kathleen and they had a big hug.

Teddy was shaking his jar noisily. "Nan, you can have black, blue, light blue, pink. You can't have orange because Teddy stood on them." "What!?" said mum jumping out of her seat "Where? What has he done?" "On the kitchen floor" said Tommy. "There's a mess". Mum headed quickly for the kitchen.

Nan and Kathleen looked at each other when she was gone. "Was that our shopping trip?" said Kathleen. "I think it was." said Nan. "Maybe the rosary beads will be nice." whispered Kathleen "I'd really like some sparkly lilac ones. Maybe Mum has found some like that." They could hear mum vacuuming while Tommy and Teddy fought about who could keep the orange capsules. "Maybe." said Nan but she did not look hopeful. Kathleen was concerned. "Nan, I don't want Jesus to be disappointed." she said. Just then Mum came back in.

"OK." she said "Here come the rosary beads." The rosaries appeared on the screen. Kathleen could see fifteen very similar shots of plain brown wooden beads. Again, every one had its own story. There were no colours apart from brown and there was nothing sparkly. Kathleen chose a set made by nuns who lived in a convent built in the middle of a sustainable forest in the Wicklow mountains. There were no boards for tiaras or jewellery but by now everyone was rather tired.

"I have a surprise!" said Mum walking out of the room. Kathleen and Nan looked at each other with a mixture of hope and suspicion. Tommy and Teddy who had been building a robot from orange capsules sat up and stared at the kitchen door waiting for Mum's return.

"Cakes, cakes, cakes!" said Teddy who was the first to see what Mum had. "Oooooooh!" said everyone else.   Mum was holding a tray piled with eclairs, cupcakes and muffins. "I know you ladies like the Café Kylemore when you go shopping" said Mum "so I stocked up."   "Wow, thanks Mum" said Kathleen "You're the world's best at online shopping!"

Chapter 6

Super Saturday

The first thing Kathleen always did on Saturday morning was to walk outside to the post box to collect the Examiner for her dad. As she gathered the sections together and tried to stop the magazines from falling out Kathleen suddenly froze. She had just seen something amazing. Hugging the papers to her chest she ran up the drive.

Breakfast with Kathleen O'Brien's family was always noisy. Dad was making the Saturday Fry-Up. Tommy and Teddy were shouting their orders and then changing their minds and shouting new orders. Mum was reading her celebrity horoscope magazine and ignoring everyone.

Tommy was holding a banana to his ear and shouting "Hello, Banana! Hello! No-one is listening to me and all I want is four sausages and one black pudding and two rashers. That's not much to ask, is it, Banana?"

Teddy was pulling on mum's sleeve and complaining. "Mum ! Tell Dad I want four sausages and two black puddings no three no four black puddings and and and …hang on five sausages and.. Mum! Mum!"

Without taking her eyes off her magazine mum ruffled Teddy's hair. "Are you wasting away? Is Daddy starving you?"

Dad looked up from chopping black pudding to try to calm things down. "You'll get what I give you or you'll be fat as fools. Tommyy, eat the banana or put it back in the bowl. Teddy, will you give your mother some peace."

Kathleen appeared at the door. Her eyes were bright with excitement. She placed the newspaper on her Dad's chair but held onto the Super Saturday magazine.

She had spotted something – an advertisement for rosary beads. There was a little photo showing strings of beads on a white cushion. They were all different colours – white, blue, pink and …..lilac! There they were. Exactly the ones she wanted.

Tommy and Teddy had jumped out of their seats and were scattering sections of the newspaper while they hunted for the comics.

Kathleen took the advertisement to her mum. "Look, Mum" she said excitedly "You can get lilac rosary beads. On Cook Street. There's a shop…" Tommy shouted over her. "Ha ha ha. I have the comics. Go on, Teddy. You can read the farming page. Find out what you should be feeding your pigs." Mum said sternly "Boys! Pick up the papers. What's that, Kathleen? Boys! Now!"

Kathleen carried on. "You see, Luke and Jack have pink as their colour scheme and if I had a lilac rosary then I'd be different and .." Teddy butted in. "Mum, that's not fair. Tommy has the comics. Tell him to give me half."

Tommy had thrown the comics on the ground and grabbed Kathleen's Super Saturday magazine. "Look! He shouted "It's Claire!" He was right. There on the front cover of the Super Saturday magazine, just above the rosary beads, was a photo of cousin Claire and her car.

The car had once been an ordinary car but Claire had decorated it. It was bright pink like a piece of bubble gum. There was pink fur all around the steering wheel. The gear stick was covered in mock diamonds. There was even a lemonade bar in the glove compartment with tiny bottles of pink lemonade. "Wow!" Tommy shouted. "Claire is going to be on telly! She's going to be on Bling Yer Wheels".

Dad stopped chopping. Mum looked up from her magazine. Everyone was trying to look at the picture and read about Claire and her car. Teddy was too short to see. He reached up to pull the picture nearer and accidentally ripped it in two.

Claire was on her own now. Her car was on a strip of paper in Teddy's hand. Dad looked very grumpy. "Right! Now!" he said crossly. "Sit down the lot of ye! Ye're all annoying me. Your mum will put the picture on the fridge where ye can all see it AFTER I've read it.

Everyone had forgotten about Kathleen's rosary beads. The advertisement had been torn in two and was lying under mum's shoe. But Kathleen was smiling to herself. She had a brilliant

idea. She knew how to show Jesus she was
making an effort. She decided to Bling her Beads!!

Chapter 7

The Holy Communion Clean-Up

It was only a week to the big day. Kathleen's mum and Maureen's mum were chatting at the school gate. Maureen's mum was talking excitedly about something while rooting in her handbag. Eventually she pulled out a little business card with the logo G G stamped on one side in shiny gold letters. Kathleen's mum placed it carefully in her bag.

As Kathleen was about to get in the car Maureen ran up to her. "You forgot your peann luaidh." she said handing Kathleen a short chewed up pencil. Kathleen was about to protest that the pencil wasn't hers but Maureen whispered "I need to warn you about them. They are dangerous. Don't say I was talking to you. " She ran off.

That evening Kathleen heard her mum on the phone to Nan Knowles. "I have found a wonderful company to do the Communion Clean-Up. They are called Glan agus Gone. They clean the house completely and get rid of all the sentimental clutter that is lying around blocking the flow of energy. And they give things to charity."

At school the next day Maureen and Kathleen met in a quiet corner of the playground. "They throw out old toys." said Maureen wide-eyed and worried. "But I don't mind that." said Kathleen. I have a lot of pink toys that Tommy and Teddy won't play with. I don't mind the charity shops having my old Tutti Cutie Computer or my Pinkie Winkie Blinkie Flashing Light Mobile.

"That's not what I mean. Look in here. " said Maureen opening her school bag. Inside were three battered Barbies. One had only one arm. The other two were covered in blue marker. "They try to throw out the things the charity shops won't want. But I love my Barbie, Barbee and Barbi so I've hidden them in my schoolbag. They take toys with missing legs or wheels or hair and put them in a skip."

"What!?" said Kathleen, scared now. "Would they take Frumpy and Frowsy?". "They would!" said Maureen. Frumpy and Frowsy were Kathleen's two My Little Ponies. They once had long flowing manes and tails but not any more. Tommy and Teddy had chopped their hair off to make Dad a wig for Father's Day.

"Glan agus Gone make a big fuss of the donations they make to the charity shops" said Maureen "but my Barbies and your ponies are no use to them so they put them in the skip. Hide them!"

The following Saturday the ladies from Glan agus Gone were talking to Mum about their cleaning strategy. "We find that with boys' rooms it's best to use these." said one of the ladies. She handed mum two signs, one saying "STAY OUT!" and another saying "DANGER!".

The ladies had been busy clearing clutter and carrying the clutter bags out to their van. The good toys went into a bag and so did many of Mum and Dad's old clothes, shoes, bags and ornaments. There was a skip in the garden with a heap of old and broken things. Tommy and Teddy were standing on tippy toes to see what was in there.

Kathleen was in her bedroom doing homework and keeping her schoolbag close.

Mum's phone rang. "Oh hello, Mam" she said. "The clean up is nearly done. Can you come round soon to look after Kathleen while I head into town with the boys. The man will come for the skip in about half an hour. I'm delighted to have that job done."

Nan arrived twenty minutes later. "OK, Kathleen." she said. "Let's see what they've done". Nan walked around the house with her hands on her hips and her eyes narrowed. She did not look impressed. She ran a finger along the phone table. She showed Kathleen the dust on her fingertip.

"There's only one thing for this." she said "I'm calling The Girls". She found her mobile phone and rang her friends. "Right." she said. "Lorraine is waiting for a cake to come out of the oven but Sheila, Peggy, Muriel and Patricia are on their way now." Kathleen and Nan sat down to have a few Fig Rolls and waited for The Girls. Soon there were two mobility scooters parked outside and a Zimmer frame in the hall. The Girls were pulling on different coloured rubber gloves.

"Anyone for tea?" asked Nan. "No, we'll get straight to it" said Patricia. "I'll start on the woodwork." "And I'm doing the bathrooms " said Sheila. "I'll help you." said Muriel, "Come here to me, Sheila." said Muriel "Did Danny ever get his ulcer sorted?" Oh, don't talk to me about ulcers." said Sheila as they headed for the upstairs bathroom. An hour later they were still talking about ulcers while the bathroom sparkled. Nan was polishing all the brass and silver. Kathleen was helping Peggy to sandpaper the coffee table.

"Were you shopping in Douglas?" asked Patricia, as she dusted the hall table. She picked up the Glan agus Gone card with its two gold Gs. "I've had some lovely scarves from this place". Nan looked puzzled. "Scarves from cleaners?? What do you mean?" she asked.   "No, no" said

Patricia. "GG is Gigi's Glories a fabulous second-hand and vintage shop. They do clothes, shoes, bags, ornaments, toys. Lovely stuff."

The bell rang. It was Lorraine with her cake in one hand and purple rubber gloves in the other. "What's going on here?" she asked pointing at the crowd behind her.

Kathleen had been so worried about her ponies that she had forgotten to tell Nan that Tommy and Teddy were not in town with mum. They had stayed behind to look at the skip and they must have climbed in to have a look.

The man who had come for the skip was shouting "I can't take a skip with boys in it. We don't take boys". "Oh dear' sighed Nan "Well, if he won't I suppose we'll have to. Come on, Kathleen. Let's go and rescue your brothers."

Chapter 8

Blinging the Beads

Blinging wasn't easy. If Kathleen was an only child she could ask her mum or dad to buy her some glitter glues. Then she could easily decorate her rosary beads. However, in this family Tommy and Teddy would want a present too. That meant that a two euro present would cost her mum six euro so usually Kathleen didn't bother asking. Brothers were pests.

But Kathleen had a plan. Unusually for a little girl she had a paid job. Every time she collected a lollipop stick that had been dropped by the boys, or even herself, her dad would give her ten cents. The lollipop sticks might land on the seat of the car, or on the living room carpet or in the drive. Dad hated them. He called them "disgusting, sticky yokes" and he was happy to pay her to get rid of them.   So far she had saved up three euro and ten cents. She had hoped to buy a new My Little Pony but the rosary was more important. She counted out two euro and fifty cents and placed it carefully in her schoolbag. She was going to buy glitter glues from a boy in her class, Damien.

The next day she handed the cash to Luke. Luke was going to give two euro and 25 cents to Damien in return for a packet of glitter glues. The glitter glues cost two euro but Damien was getting 25 cents profit. Luke was getting also 25 cents. That was his payment for talking to Damien. Damien did not like having anything to do with girls. He was rude and unfriendly but he did have a lot of art materials so this way of working suited everyone.

Luke went up to him at playtime. Damien glared at him "Are you yourself or are you the other fella?" he asked suspiciously. Luke was used to being confused with his twin brother. "I'm myself." he said "I'm Luke." The boys swapped their items. To be fair to Damien he kept his things in good condition. The tubes of glitter glue were mostly full and all very clean.

Kathleen got to work that evening after school. She took out the glitter glues and her wooden beads. She was going to think about stories from the four different Mysteries of the Rosary and that would help her to decide what colours to use.

The Joyful Mysteries should be pink and red and orange. She would do ten of them. The Sorrowful Mysteries would be blue because Jesus must have felt blue carrying that heavy cross. Two of them. The Glorious Mysteries could be purple and gold…twelve of them.

The Luminous Mysteries could be white and bright…maybe yellow. Kathleen's Granddad had told her the story of the Wedding Feast at Cana where Jesus had turned water into wine after the host had run out. Maybe the beads should be wine coloured. Her mum's favourite was pink champagne …It was a wedding so chances are that Jesus would have made pink champagne. She finished the rosary with Wedding Feast of Cana pink champagne beads.

She said a little prayer to Jesus asking him to make sure they didn't run out of wine or lemonade on the day of the party.

Her hands were covered in glitter glue …there was glitter all over the rug but these beads looked fabulous.

Mum tapped on her bedroom door. "What are you up to, love?" she asked. Kathleen held up the beads proudly. But then things took a bad turn. Instead of being impressed mum looked upset.

"Oh, Kathleen." she said sounding stressed out. "You've ruined the beads. You can never take them into a church like that. I hope your Nan has some spare ones". She walked out holding the beads and tutting.

This was awful. After all her hard work and effort Kathleen had absolutely nothing to show for it. Her beads were gone. Her money was gone. Her hopes of a new My Little Pony were gone and she had nothing for Show and Tell the next day. She fell asleep with tears rolling down her face.

Chapter 9

Show and Tell

When Kathleen's mum dropped her and Tommy to school there was great excitement going on. Cars were parked outside the school but people had walked next door to look at the church. The school secretary, Siobhan, handed Kathleen's mum a leaflet. It was the school newsletter. Usually it was full of little news items like schoolbook sales, swimming lessons and nits but today there was only one news item. The headline said"Wrecking Ball Accident in the Churchyard". It turned out that the builders had had a little accident the night before. Father Hearty had called them in to smarten up the building and now there was huge hole outside the front entrance.

Kathleen's mum stepped out of the car to chat to Siobhan. "Have a little peek in the gate." said Siobhan. "I'll keep an eye on your gang." Kathleen's Mum came back shaking her head. "It's like a bomb fell!" she said. Siobhan explained to her that babies might have to be carried into the Communion and that toddlers like Teddy might have to walk into the church instead of using their buggies. "Can you manage a few steps?" she asked Teddy. He went all shy and hid behind Tommy. "Father Hearty is talking to the builders." said Siobhan. "I'll text everyone tonight with any updates".

"But, Mum" said Kathleen worried. "What about Granddad? He can't walk a few steps, can he?" "We'll see what Father Hearty says." said Kathleen's mum. "Go on, kids, go on into school." Kathleen was very concerned. Teddy could take care of himself but what about Granddad?

Miss Cronin was standing at the classroom door. A big sign on the door said "Holy Communion Show and Tell Day".

Show and Tell Day was Miss Cronin's idea. She knew that Holy Communion Days were full of beautiful, new, exciting things. If you weren't careful the new beads and books and bracelets and presents might distract the children during the mass. On Show and Tell Day the class would get a look at the distracting things in advance. That meant they would be able to concentrate on making their Communions. Miss Cronin had told all the children to bring in their special possessions and anything else they wanted to show off. Later on the Fifth Class choir were going to come in and sing the songs they had learned. It was a busy day full of noise and fun......good preparation for the serious ceremony tomorrow.

It was Jack and Luke's turn for Show and Tell. Father Hearty was letting them do a performance after the Fifth Class choir sang. Jack was doing his Communion dance while Luke did a rap.

"And they'll know we are Christians by our love, love, love." rapped Luke while Jack did his hip hop moves. The whole class gave a round of applause and cheered.

Miss Cronin admired the boys' new short haircuts. "Your buzzcuts look extremely smart." she said. Luke explained "We wanted to have Jedward hairstyles but mum said we must wait til we're older. For our confirmations, maybe". "Or our weddings." added Jack".

Everyone had something nice. Many of the boys had new watches. A lot of the girls had crucifixes on silver chains. Nessa had a Communion Copter to bring her to the church and Gillian had a snow-shaker of Jesus that her aunt had sent from Spain.

Everyone was applauding Damien. He had done a huge drawing that was going to hang in the church. It showed the Baby Jesus being rescued from a shark by a horse and her foal. Miss Cronin thanked God for Damien's imagination and skill.

It was Nessa's turn. Nessa was talking about how the Communion Copter was a little white and silver chopper painted with a picture of her as a super heroine. Father Hearty had given special permission for it to land behind the church. "So while you are all driving to the church" Nessa said proudly "I will be overhead in my special copter looking down on you all." Jack nudged Luke. "She doesn't need a helicopter to look down on us." he whispered. Nessa was still going on "Then I'll fly home to open my presents, have my face painted and bounce on my three bouncy castles."

"Thank you, Nessa." said Miss Cronin. "Let's thank God for all the employment your party will provide."

It was Kathleen's turn. She stood up at the top of the class with a little Dunnes bag. "I'm going to talk about the vest my Granddad bought for me." she said.

Just then there was a huge bang from the churchyard. "Oh, dear" said Miss Cronin. "Sorry about this, Kathleen. I need Ciúnas from you all for five minutes while I see what's wrong."

Nessa took her chance to pick on Kathleen. "Imagine bringing a vest to Show and Tell" she said nastily. "I don't think Jesus will be very impressed. Don't you have anything proper like my Communion Copter?" Kathleen looked her in the eye. "I'm happy with this." she said quietly. Nessa went on. "I thought you liked praying, Kathleen. Why didn't you pray for something better than that. I'd be disgusted if someone gave me a vest."

It was all too much for Kathleen. She put her Dunnes bag on the desk and marched up to Nessa. "Shut up!" she said "Just shut up! My Granddad gave me my vest. Don't you ever insult my Granddad again or I'll push you into the River Lee." Nessa was still banging on. "Well, I think a vest is pathetic I'm getting a bracelet, a new TV, a box of ...."

"Stop!" shouted Kathleen. "Will you just stop! Communion is wasted on you. At Easter you didn't listen to any of the stories about Jesus. All you wanted to do was make your Dad buy you more and more chocolate eggs 'til you threw up And at Christmas you didn't even look at the crib, you just whined about presents. Now all you talk about is helicopters and castles. You are missing the point same as you always do. The reason we get nice things is to show Jesus we care, not to show off."

"I'm ringing my Dad." said Nessa. "He'll sort you out." She was the only child in the class with a mobile phone.

She began banging numbers into her phone. Kathleen held out her hand. "Yes, I'd like to talk to your dad. I'd like to talk to him about texting in the church and yawning and looking around him during mass. He is so rude to Father Hearty and to Jesus. Hand him over." Nessa blushed red and put her phone back in her pocket.

Before Nessa could reply Miss Cronin came back in. "Oh dear, the florist crashed her car into the church gate. The debris from the wrecking ball burst her tyre and she skidded. I don't know if we'll have any flowers tomorrow."

All the children were shocked into silence by the row. Miss Cronin looked surprised…"My goodness, ye are all very quiet. Kathleen, come and tell us all about your pretty vest."

Kathleen took a deep breath. She explained how her vest had a heart pattern because her Granddad loved her very much and he would be close to her heart on the Communion Day even if he could not get into the church. "Lovely!" said Miss Cronin "And did you know that one of the names for Jesus is the Sacred Heart? Let's thank him for Kathleen's Granddad and all our families. Let's pray we all have a great day tomorrow"

Chapter 10

Dresses

It was the night before the Communion. With all the fuss about the hole in the churchyard Kathleen never got a chance to tell anyone abut the row with Nessa. It was too late now for confession. She didn't know what to do. What if Nessa's dad made a fuss?

Nan and Granddad were staying over. There was no way of getting Granddad into the church so this was the best way to include him in the day. At tea time everyone was talking about the state of the church. "No flowers. A huge hole in the yard" said Nan. "I wonder if I should wear my combat trousers to go in there" "Poor Father Hearty." said Mum. "He will be mortified. He always has the church looking lovely for the Communions. I remember he had it gorgeous on my Communion day all those years ago." "That was a mighty day." said Granddad. "Why don't you have the photos hanging up?" "Oh, no reason." said Mum looking uncomfortable.

Kathleen realised she had never seem Mum's Communion photo. There was a picture of Dad in a purple velvet jacket and a ruffled shirt on the mantlepiece but none of Mum. "Mum," said Kathleen "What was your communion dress like?" "Oh, it was horrible" said mum "Not tasteful at all. I looked awful".

"INDEED, YOU DID NOT!" said Nan Knowles. Granddad, Mum and Kathleen jumped. Nan Knowles never shouted. She was rooting furiously in her bag. She reached in and took out an old photo hidden in her purse. "It's me!" said Mum "on my First Holy Communion day." "Remember you were the first girl in Cork to have cornrows and ringlets in the one hairstyle?" said

Nan proudly.   And the first to have FOUR hoops in her dress! " added Granddad. "Do you remember the teacher had to cut one of your petticoats so you could walk" "Yes." said Mum "My high heels got caught up in the cloth and I couldn't move." She was staring at the photo.

"And do you remember me trying to control that mad pony that pulled your sulky to the church?" asked Granddad. "Poor Shamrock." said Mum 'Will I ever forget?" "Yes." said Granddad. "We nearly lost you when he took off at Shea's pub and if it weren't for the road bowlers blocking his way you'd have ended up in Macroom the speed we were going." "But I'll tell you something. " added Nan "Your three-tier-tiara never slipped." "But I wasn't tasteful at all." said Mum.

"Tasteful?" said Granddad "Sure, don't mind tasteful. What's tasteful only being the same as everyone else and boring? You were the most lovely girl in the church. When you sang people had tears in their eyes. Do you remember when they did the Sign of Peace you got up out of your seat to shake hands with everyone at the back of the church. You walked up the aisle with your hands together and all the other children followed you. Ye shook hands with everyone in the church and the priest said ye were the nearest thing to angels he had ever seen. I was so proud of you. Everyone wanted to have their picture taken with you."

"Really?" said mum "Really?" "You look brilliant, Mum." said Kathleen. 'I think you look kind of amazeballs.". Mum smiled. "You know, Kathleen, maybe your dress is a bit plain."

Mum suddenly went into a panic! Oh, Mam, Dad, Kathleen. I HAVE made an awful mistake. Kathleen asked for some sparkle and her dress is DESPERATE plain. Oh, what was I thinking?" She looked like she was going to cry.

Kathleen spoke up.

"It's OK, Mum" she said. "Jesus doesn't really mind what I wear. He'll be glad to see me in the church on the day. He's a man, like Dad or Granddad, so he probably doesn't really notice dresses.

Nan had a strange look on her face. "I might have something." she said.   She gave Granddad a wink. He winked back. "Follow me." Kathleen and Mum followed her to where her car was parked. She opened the boot. Inside was a big Monsoon bag. Mam and Kathleen were intrigued. Nan switched on the torch on her car keys and showed them what was inside. It was a sparkly dress. "It's the dress I tried on last year! You bought it!' said Kathleen.

All three of them stared. Compared with the tasteful dress this dress was glamorous and exciting. Under Nan's torch it shimmered and twinkled. "It's beautiful." said Mum. "Shall we go in and fit it on?"

Kathleen shook her head. "It's a great dress, Nan. Thank you. But Mum put lots of effort into finding the tasteful dress so I want to wear that." Mum and Nan hugged her.

"But could I wear the tiara, please?" Kathleen added. "Of course." said mum. "And your beads …let me find you a nice bag to put them in. Let's go inside. You hop into bed. I'll bring you hot chocolate and marshmallows." "Hooray!" said Kathleen and dashed off to bed happy.

Nan went to lock up the car. Her phone rang. She didn't recognize the number or the voice of the man who said hello. "Mrs Knowles.

I need to talk to you. This is Nessa's dad." "Go on." said Nan. "I'm listening"

Chapter 11

On the Day

The house was buzzing with life.   When Kathleen went for breakfast she barely recognised her own home. The aunties and uncles had arrived early to help decorate.   Auntie Dee was hanging up Happy First Holy Communion banners.   Auntie Di was tying balloons onto every tree and bush in the garden. Uncle Dave was putting a huge white bow on the garden swing. There were flowers and scented candles all over the place.

Tommy and Teddy were sitting quietly on the sofa in the conservatory. "Lads, are ye not feeling well?" asked Granddad "We're being good." said Teddy. "Shhh, Teddy! " said Tommy. "We're not acting the maggot today because Kathleen is making her Holy Credit Union"

Dad was doing a special version of the Saturday Fry Up. He called Auntie Dee, Auntie Di and Uncle Dave in from the garden. There were three frying pans on the hob. One big one for Auntie Dee and Uncle Dave who were working hard plus a vegetarian one for Auntie Di. They marched in and shouted out orders. They looked like scruffy workmen in their jeans and sweatshirts.

"Are you guys worried about going out dressed like that?" asked Dad. "Why so?" asked Auntie Dee. "Aren't you afraid RTE might want to film you for their style section?" Everyone laughed. Dad was very proud of the fact that Mum had been stopped twice by RTE because of her lovely clothes. They filmed her for a fashion program explaining where she had got the beautiful things she was wearing.

"Where are the ladies now? " asked Auntie Di. "Flew away." said Teddy. "Shhhh, Teddy!"

said Tommy. Just then Mum knocked on the kitchen door. "Holy Communion girl coming through" she shouted. Everyone watched the door as Mum opened it wide and beckoned Kathleen in. Everyone cheered and clapped. "Tissues!" shouted the aunties "Has anyone got tissues?" All the aunties were crying and Dad was rubbing his eyes. "Unbelievable" said Di, "Stunning" said Dee, "Grand" said Dave.

Kathleen looked amazing. With her long legs and slim build she cut an elegant figure. The dress which looked straight and plain on the hanger was stylish and refined once Kathleen put it on. Mum had placed the beads in a see-through chiffon pocket sewn neatly onto Kathleen's bag. They added a discrete splash of colour.

"Come here, love." said Granddad. "Here's something for you." He held up a beautiful white gold necklace with a cross and put it around

Kathleen's neck. "I did some internet shopping myself." he explained. Kathleen threw her arms around him. "I wish you were coming." she said.

Suddenly everyone got busy. Dad grabbed the camera and took Kathleen to the garden for photos. When they came back in the aunties and uncle had been transformed. The work clothes were gone and they looked super smart in high heels, a suit and glammy make up. "You get some style from this side of the family too, Kathleen" said Auntie Dee.

Dad looked stunned. "You're coming to mass?" he asked ""But you haven't been to mass since ye came to my wedding." Dee, Di and Dave shrugged. "Well, we're coming along now. For Kathleen."

Kathleen had something in her hand, "Is this for Father Hearty?" she asked holding up a twenty euro note. "Mrs Cotter next door just put it in my bag." Everyone laughed. "Ah, bless". said Auntie Di. Kathleen decided to check again later.

Uncle Dave gave a shout."Hey, have you seen the time? Come on everyone, cars! I'll take these two." he shouted scooping up Teddy and putting Tommy onto his shoulders. All the cars headed for the church. "Take plenty pictures for me." said Granddad. "I'll be back as quick as I can." said Kathleen hugging him goodbye.

Kathleen's Mum helped her into the back seat and off they went. The sun was shining without a cloud in the sky. "Is that your friend's copter?" asked Dad. Kathleen looked out " I don't think so, Dad. It's black and hers is white. And there's two of them. No, three."

They parked outside the church, next door to the school. The churchyard was heaving with girls in white, smart lads in suits and everyone else in their colourful Sunday best. Father Hearty suddenly appeared with two huge flags. "Welcome everyone, can ye all stand over here because…" Whatever he said next was drowned out by the roar of helicopters. A fleet of twenty black choppers was making straight for the church. Everyone huddled together and stared.

The helicopters were hovering in a circle over the church. Simultaneously every chopper cast out a long rope ladder. Men in black were climbing down the ladders at speed. A strange assortment of items was being lowered on ropes into the yard; mysterious packages of all sizes. The children were too fascinated to be scared. "They're fixing the hole." said Kathleen's Dad. "More than that." said Mum. "They're decorating."

The men had created a temporary driveway into the church and other men were rolling out a thick cream and white carpet. Gold embroidery on the carpet spelled out the words "Welcome to the House of God." Six men rolled it along the driveway and into the church. Six other men were attaching huge, tall bunches of white and gold flowers to every pew. A mixture of flowers and fibre optics made each bouquet shimmer and glow.

Four men in black were doing special effects. White fire fountains appeared all around the edge of the churchyard. A light show of dancing crosses was being projected onto the church walls. The helicopters circling the church suddenly lowered their ladders. The men were pulled back on board and the helicopters sped off. Six more black helicopters approached flying close together. As they approached the church they split up to reveal a little white chopper decorated with a pattern of silver crosses. "Is THAT your friend's chopper?" asked Dad. "It can't be." said

Kathleen, puzzled. "She's over there." Nessa was over by the gate with her dad. The two of them were grinning and waving at Kathleen.

The chopper was coming down, creating huge gusts of wind. All the girls grabbed their veils while the ladies held onto their hats. The doors opened and Kathleen screamed. It was Granddad. He wasn't stuck at home. He was right here. Nan Knowles was right beside him. "Surprise!" they shouted. Nessa's dad came over to shake their hands. "Good landing, chaps!" he said. He shook Father Hearty's hand with both his hands. Two men in black grabbed the wheelchair and raced into the church along the luxury carpet. Nessa ran up to Kathleen. "Are you happy?" she asked "I got the point of Communion. If Jesus had a helicopter he would have lent it to your Granddad." Kathleen nodded. She was too happy to speak.

Nessa and her dad went off hand in hand grinning. Kathleen's family gathered around her. Everyone in the churchyard was smiling. There was a shout from the church.

Father Hearty was standing at the new entrance. "Come on in everyone." he said. "Let's get these children into this church of ours. I think it will be a very good day"

THE END

Thank you for taking the time to read my book. I hope you enjoyed reading about Kathleen and her family in Cork.

If you'd like to find out more about me and my books, you can find me on Smashwords:

https://www.smashwords.com/profile/view/AvrilFrances

Or write to me:

avrilfrances@hotmail.com